THE

Tim Collins

Illustrated by James Lawrence

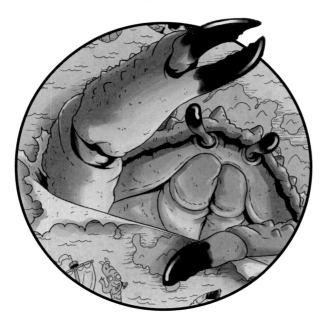

5106 845

Titles in Monster Island:

THE APE
TIM COLLINS & ABBY RYDER

THE DINOSAUR
TIM COLLINS & JAMES LAWRENCE

THE SQUID
TIM COLLINS & JAMES LAWRENCE

THE YETI
TIM COLLINS & ABBY RYDER

THE CRAB
TIM COLLINS & JAMES LAWRENCE

THE CYCLOPS
TIM COLLINS & ABBY RYDER

Badger Publishing Limited, Oldmedow Road,
Hardwick Industrial Estate, King's Lynn PE30 4JJ

Telephone: 01438 791037
www.badgerlearning.co.uk

The Crab ISBN 978-1-78837-350-0

2 4 6 8 10 9 7 5 3 1

Publisher / Senior Editor: Danny Pearson
Editor: Claire Morgan
Series Consultant: Dee Reid
Designer: Fiona Grant
Cover Illustration: Mark Penman
Illustration: James Lawrence

THE CRAB

Tim Collins

Illustrated by James Lawrence

Contents

Story Vocabulary

rescue

pouring

answer

The story so far...

Mina and Yasmin were stuck on the island. They walked along the beach.

"Welcome to Monster Island," said a man. "I am the Captain. You will never escape."

Mina and Yasmin laughed. They thought the Captain was mad.

"Why is it called Monster Island?" asked Mina.

"You will soon find out," said the Captain.

Chapter 1
Help

"We must get away," said Mina.

Yasmin saw some rocks.

"We could use the rocks to spell out the word 'HELP'," she said. "A plane might see it and rescue us."

"OK!" said Mina.

But she didn't think it was a good idea.

She hadn't seen any planes flying over the island.

The girls heard someone laughing.

It was the Captain. "That plan will never work," he said.

"Yes it will," said Yasmin.

Mina and Yasmin picked up one of the big rocks.

They began to carry it over the sand.

It was hard work.

Suddenly, Yasmin screamed. She let go of the rock.

"What are you doing?" cried Mina.
"The rock nearly fell on my foot!"

Yasmin was holding her right foot.

It was pouring with blood.

"It was that crab," said Yasmin.
"It pinched my foot."

Mina saw a small red crab.

There was blood on its claw.

Chapter 2

Warning

Mina picked up a rock.

She was going to scare off the small crab before it could attack them again.

"That would be a big mistake," said
a voice.

Mina turned around.

It was the Captain.

"If you do that, it will make her angry,"
he said.

"You are mad!" said Mina. "It will be scared, not angry."

She threw the rock at the crab.

It ran off into the sea.

"Good. It's gone now," said Mina.

She turned back to Yasmin. "How is your foot?" she asked.

But Yasmin didn't answer.

She was looking at the sea.

"Look at that!" she said.

Mina looked at the sea.

A huge monster was coming out of the waves.

It was a giant red crab.

It was coming for Mina and Yasmin,
snapping its huge claws.

"Run!" shouted Mina.

Chapter 3

Revenge

The giant crab ran at Mina and Yasmin.

"You go on!" yelled Yasmin. "My foot hurts too much to run."

"No!" shouted Mina.

She grabbed Yasmin and helped her across the beach.

If we can get to the trees, we will be safe, thought Mina.

Mina ran as fast as she could, but she was getting tired.

"Just leave me," said Yasmin.

"No way!" said Mina.

But the monster was getting closer and closer.

The monster's huge claw was reaching out for Mina's leg.

"Ha! Ha! Ha!" laughed the Captain. "I did warn you."

Then Mina felt a sharp pain in her leg.

The crab's huge claw had grabbed her.

The crab began to drag Mina away.

"No!" yelled Yasmin.

But she couldn't stop the monster.

Mina screamed and screamed as the giant crab dragged her away towards the sea. Then she was gone.

Just then, Yasmin heard a sound in the sky. It was a plane flying over the island.

Ape Mountain

Yeti Cave

Crab Cove

Dinosaur Pen

Cyclops Forest

Squid Sea

SQUID INK

Questions

Chapter 1

What does Yasmin plan to do with the rocks? *(page 6)*

Why does Yasmin drop the rock? *(page 12)*

Chapter 2

Who warns Mina about the giant crab? *(page 14)*

What do Mina and Yasmin see coming out of the waves? *(page 21)*

Chapter 3

What does the Captain do when he sees Mina and Yasmin in trouble? *(page 26)*

What do you think Yasmin will do now?

About the Author

Tim Collins has written over 70 books for children and adults.

He lives near Oxford and spends his time listening to rock music and playing Pokémon.

He went to a real desert island once, but he didn't see any monsters.

About the Illustrator

James Lawrence loves reading comic books.

He lives in Manchester and he spends his days drawing cool pictures.

He thinks he could be friends with the Captain.